Soore im

in

scool

Bate

Tok

Hi

You

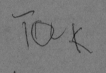

TABLE OF CONTENTS

Ahoy, mateys! Do you want to join my pirate crew? Then just say the pirate password: "Yo-ho-ho!" As part of my crew, you'll need to learn the Never Land pirate pledge.

Today's Pirate Pledge

A good pirate always shares with his mateys.

X MARKS THE CROC!

ADAPTED BY MELINDA LAROSE
BASED ON THE EPISODE "ROCK THE CROC"
WRITTEN BY MIKE RAAB
ILLUSTRATED BY ALAN BATSON

Disney PRESS

New York • Los Angeles

The 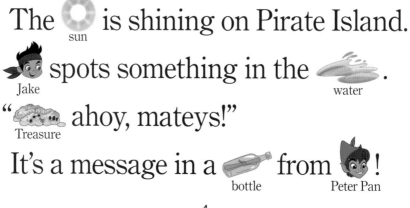sun is shining on Pirate Island.

Jake spots something in the water.

"Treasure ahoy, mateys!"

It's a message in a bottle from Peter Pan!

4

"A  of Pirates' Plunge!" says Cubby.

"Pirates' Plunge is the coolest waterslide in all of Never Land," says Jake.

"Yo-ho, let's go!" says Izzy.

Can you find Bucky on the map?

"There's 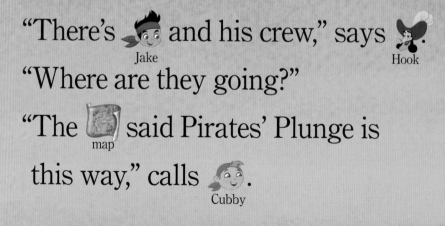 and his crew," says 🎩.
Jake   Hook

"Where are they going?"

"The 📜 said Pirates' Plunge is
map

this way," calls 👦.
Cubby

"Pirates' Plunge?" asks  .
Hook
"Of course! Those puny pirates
are going to cool off on the  .
waterslide
 , I want that  !"
Smee   map

How many coconuts
can you find on
the beach?

Yoink!  nabs the map.
Hook

"Yay-hey, no way!" shouts Izzy.

"Don't swipe our map," says Jake.

"Let's go to Pirates' Plunge together!"

"Together? Never!" says .
Hook

"I want the place all to myself!"

tries to grab the back.
Jake   bottle

It goes flying into the sky!

"Shiver me timbers," says  Izzy.
"The Croc ate the map!"
"Aww, coconuts!" says Cubby. "Now no one
can go to Pirates' Plunge."

10

Just then, a  feather lands on Cubby's nose.

"Ahh…ahhh…CHOO!"

"That's it!" says Jake. "We can get the Croc to sneeze out the map!"

Can you help Jake spot the crocodile?

The crew finds the  sleeping.
Croc

"Maybe he will sneeze if we tickle

his nose with a 🪶," says 🏴‍☠️.
feather   Jake

"Worked for me," says 😊.
Cubby

AHH
AHH
AHH

[Skully] tickles the [Croc's] nose.

"Ahh…ahhh…ahhh…"

"Get set to catch the [map]," says [Jake].

But the [Croc] doesn't sneeze!

"Step aside, silly swabs," says .
Hook

He rubs a ✒ feather on the 🐊 Croc's nose.

"Gootchy-gootchy-goo!"

But the 🐊 Croc doesn't sneeze!

"Why didn't it work, Smee?"

 asks.
Hook

"I don't…ahhh…ahhh…CHOO!"

 sneezes and wakes up the !
Smee   Croc

"Save me, !" yells .
Smee   Hook

He runs off.

Just then,  and  hear a burp.
Jake   Izzy

"Excuse me," says .
Cubby

"Great thinking, ," says .
Cubby   Izzy

BURP!

"Maybe we can make the  Croc burp out the map," says Jake.

"The fizzy water at Geyser Gulch makes me burp," says Izzy.

"Hey, Croc, want a drink of water?"

"The 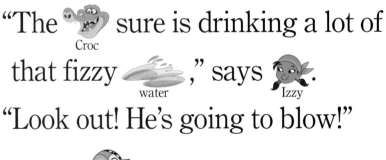 sure is drinking a lot of
Croc
that fizzy ," says .
water   Izzy
"Look out! He's going to blow!"

warns .
Skully

"Get set to catch the ," says Jake.
The Croc lets out a teeny-tiny burp.
"That's it?" says Cubby.

BURP!

How many gushing geysers do you see?

"I'll make the  burp," says .
Croc   Hook

 pats the  tummy, but
Hook   Croc's

the  doesn't like it one bit.
Croc

The  sends  flying!
Croc   Hook

"Smeeeeeee!" yells  Hook.

"Flap your arms, Cap'n," says  Smee.

"Always works for me," says  Skully.

 Cubby giggles at  Skully's joke.

", you're full of ideas," says .
Cubby   Jake

"I am?" asks .
Cubby

"Maybe we can make the  laugh
Croc

out the ," says .
map   Jake

22

"A ha-ha-ha and hee-hee-hee. Come on, 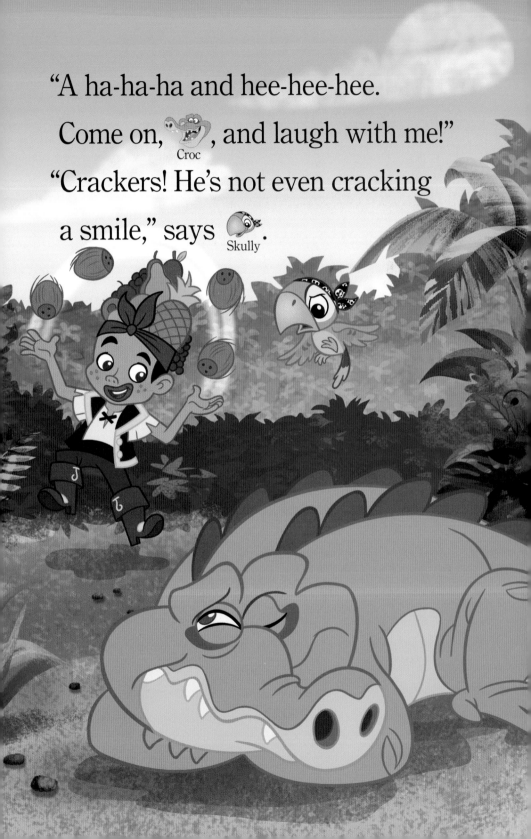 Croc, and laugh with me!"

"Crackers! He's not even cracking a smile," says Skully.

"I'll show you how it's done," says .

Hook clowns around, but the Croc still doesn't laugh.

What colors do you see on Hook's clown suit?

24

"Give me my crocodile ,"
yells  Hook. "I want that  map!"
"We all want the  map," says  Jake,
"but trapping the  Croc isn't right."

", a little ⬤ Pixie Dust, please," says 🧒 Jake.

🧒 Jake takes the 🕸 net from 🎅 Smee.

"Give me back my 🕸 net!" yells 🏴‍☠️ Hook.

 drops the net, and Hook gets all tangled up.

"Uh-oh, sorry, Hook," says Jake.

"Get me out of this !" calls Hook.

He steps on a log.

The Croc hits the log, and Hook goes flying. "Whoooooaaaa!"

"The  is laughing!" says .
Croc   Jake

The  with the  flies out of
bottle   map

the  mouth.
Croc's

"Yo-ho, way to go!" says .
Jake

Can you spot
Captain Hook and
Mr. Smee?

" was right! Pirates' Plunge is
awesome!" says .

"Too bad  tried to swipe our ,"
says .

"If that sneaky snook had shared,

he would be in the 🌊 instead
            water

of up a 🌴," says 👧.
         tree   Izzy

"For solving pirate problems,
we earned some Gold Doubloons!"
says  Jake.

"Yay-hey, well done," says Izzy.

How many Gold Doubloons did Jake and the crew earn?

Disney
DOC
McStuffins

Caught
Blue-Handed

Adapted by Sheila Sweeny Higginson
Based on the episode written by Kent Redeker
Illustrated by Alan Batson

DISNEP PRESS

New York • Los Angeles

Donny wants to show Doc the painting he made. "Guess what it is, Doc," he says to his sister.

 looks at the painting.
Doc

She does not know what it is.

"It's a blue 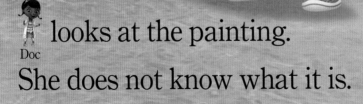 eating !"
elephant   blueberries

says .
Donny

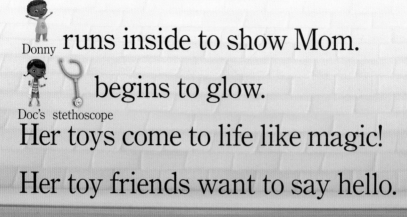

Donny runs inside to show Mom.

Doc's stethoscope begins to glow.

Her toys come to life like magic!

Her toy friends want to say hello.

 Lambie jumps up and gives Doc

a cuddle.

"It's baa-baa-beautiful to see you!"

 Lambie says.

39

Donny's toy wants to say hi, too.

He has six **hands**.

"Hiya, **Doc**!" says **Donny's** toy.

"Hi, **Glo-Bo**!" says **Doc**.

![Squeakers] hops up and gives ![Glo-Bo]
a high five.

Squeakers   Glo-Bo

"What's squeaking with my
friend?" ![Glo-Bo] asks.

Glo-Bo

pats on the back.
Glo-Bo   Surfer Girl

"How's the surf?" he asks.

"Up!" says.
          Surfer Girl

Next,  plays with  the
Glo-Bo   Buddy

dump truck.

Then he gives a big bear hug.
Chilly

That is one tight squeeze!

Then  runs back to the
Glo-Bo
painting 𝗧𝗧𝗧.
table

"I think I broke a ," says.
bone   Chilly
laughs. "Snowmen don't
Doc
have bones!"

![Chilly] doesn't have a broken ![bone].

Chilly   bone

But there is something wrong.

He has spots!

"Chilly, you need a checkup," says Doc.

Doc McStuffins will make Chilly feel better!

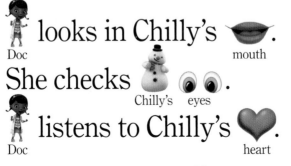

looks in Chilly's 👄.
Doc   mouth

She checks ⛄ 👀.
         Chilly's eyes

listens to Chilly's ❤️.
Doc   heart

48

 uses a ⬚ to take ⬚ temperature.
Doc   thermometer   Chilly's

"You don't have a fever, ⬚," says ⬚.
                        Chilly   Doc

"That's good."

49

"I have a diagnosis," says ![Doc] Doc.

" ![Chilly] Chilly has blue spots on his back. He has a case of mystery pox."

"Mystery pox?"  cries. "I don't
know what mystery pox is!"
"Nobody does,"  says.
"That's why it's a mystery."

 Hallie comes into  Doc's office with more patients.

 Squeakers has blue spots.

 Buddy and  Surfer Girl have blue spots, too.

"This is horrible!" says .
Chilly
Then he holds his head and faints.

Hallie steps in to catch Chilly.

Now Hallie has blue spots, too!

Doc knows how the mystery pox

is spreading now.

54

 wants to cuddle .
Lambie   Chilly

"Don't cuddle !" says .
                        Chilly   Doc

"You might get mystery pox, too!"

"Is it the end of cuddles?"  asks.
                                          Lambie

tells why she can't cuddle.
Doc   Lambie

The pox is spreading.

It is like the germs that can make

people sick.

Now has to find out who
started spreading the mystery pox.

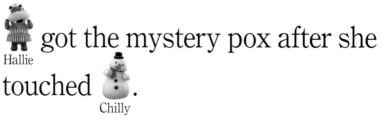 got the mystery pox after she

Hallie

touched .

Chilly

58

"Chilly, who else might have touched you?" Doc asks.

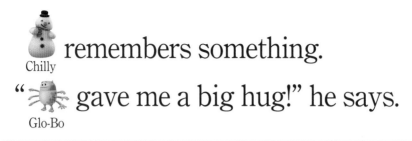 remembers something.
Chilly

" gave me a big hug!" he says.
Glo-Bo

" patted my back!" says ⟨Surfer Girl⟩.
Glo-Bo   Surfer Girl

"Me, too!" ⟨Buddy⟩ adds.
            Buddy

"That's it!" says ⟨Doc⟩. She runs to the
                   Doc

yard to find ⟨Glo-Bo⟩.
               Glo-Bo

![Doc] finds ![Glo-Bo]. He is about to

Doc   Glo-Bo

hug ![Teddy B].

Teddy B

"Stop!" she yells. "I think you're

spreading mystery pox."

 takes a close look at .
Doc   Glo-Bo

He is not sick.

But   have blue paint
   Glo-Bo's hands
on them!

"It's not mystery pox,"  says.

Doc

"It's blue paint from Glo-Bo's hands!"

"Phew!" says Chilly.

Everyone goes back to Doc's clinic.

64

The hand-washing party begins!
 washes , , and .

Doc   Glo-Bo   Chilly   Squeakers

Then she washes , , and .

Buddy   Surfer Girl   Hallie

No more mystery pox!

 has one last question.
Did you wash your  today?

Doc's Tips About Germs

- Germs can be passed from person to person.

- Germs can make you sick.

- Always sneeze into your arm or a tissue.

- Throw away your tissues after you use them.

- Cover your mouth when you cough.

- Wash your hands often, especially if you're sick.

DISNEP

Sofia the First

Sofia Makes a Friend

Written by Catherine Hapka
Illustrated by Character Building Studio
and the Disney Storybook Art Team

DISNEP PRESS

New York • Los Angeles

 is excited.
Sofia

Royal visitors are coming

to the !
palace

"King Baldric and Queen Ada will be here soon," says Queen Miranda.

"Our visitors are bringing a special guest," says King Roland. "I hope you will help her feel at home in our 🏰."

palace

"The special guest is probably a princess," Amber whispers to Sofia.

A  sounds.
trumpet

"The guests are here!" Sofia cries.

A carriage stops in front of the palace .

Two people get out of the  carriage.
"Where is the princess?" Amber
wonders.

Then a baby  jumps out of
the 🚗 !
Queen Ada smiles.

"This is our new pet .
unicorn

Her name is Pearl.

I hope you won't mind watching

her for us."

Sofia, Amber, and James take Pearl for a walk.

Pearl chases the birds and eats the flowers.

Pearl jumps into the 🔱 .
fountain

She shakes off next to Amber.

"Hey!" Amber cries. "Stop that!"

"I know," James says.

"Pearl can watch us play ."
horseshoes

He throws a .
horseshoe

Pearl catches the  and brings
horseshoe

it back to James.

"Hey! She ruined my throw!"

James says.

Amber has another idea.

"We can play dress-up.

Pearl will look cute in a pretty
 and ."
hat   tutu
Pearl takes a big bite
out of Amber's .
hat

"No, Pearl!" Amber cries.

She tries to grab the .
hat

But the  runs away.
unicorn

Pearl runs through the .
palace

She jumps on the 🎹 and nibbles
piano

on a 🖼.
tapestry

85

"Watching Pearl is no fun," James says.

"She ruins everything," Amber adds.

Pearl hears them talking.

Her head droops. Her goes dull.
horn

She runs and hides behind a .
tapestry

"We said we would help Pearl
feel at home in our  ,"
palace
 reminds the others.
Sofia

"But she does not like to do
any of the things we like to do!"
Amber says.

That gives  an idea.
Sofia

"Pearl is a ," she says.
unicorn

"We need to find out what

a  likes to do!"
unicorn

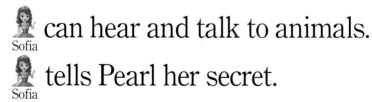 can hear and talk to animals.

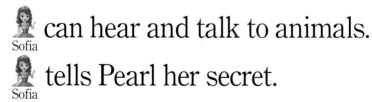 tells Pearl her secret.

"What do you like to do?" she asks.

"I love 🎵," says Pearl.

music

91

 leads the   over to
Sofia   palace   musicians

where Pearl is hiding.

The  play a lively tune.
musicians

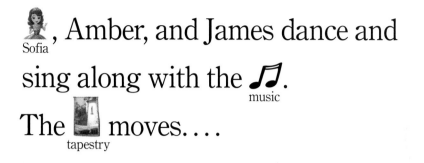 , Amber, and James dance and sing along with the . The tapestry moves....

Then Pearl jumps out!
She looks happy, and her pretty  shines again.

horn

"Hooray!"  Sofia cheers.

"We made Pearl feel at home

in our palace ."

"Because you figured out what
she likes to do."

James smiles at .

"And it's fun for us, too!"

The rest of the visit
is filled with 🎵 and fun.
music
🧒, Amber, and James can't wait
Sofia
for Pearl's next visit!

Princess Lesson

A true princess
always makes her guests
feel at home.

Sofia Takes the Lead

Written by Lisa Ann Marsoli
Based on the episode "The Buttercups," written by Doug Cooney
Illustrated by Character Building Studio
and the Disney Storybook Art Team

DISNEY PRESS

New York • Los Angeles

Sofia is a Buttercup!
Mrs. Hanshaw is her troop leader.
Today Meg and Peg join the troop.

Sofia gives the girls their vests.
"You pin badges on them," she says.

"You get badges for doing things," Jade says.

"Like swimming or picking flowers," says Ruby.

Sofia needs one more badge.
Then she will get a sunflower pin!

Tomorrow is her big chance.
The Buttercups are going on a
nature hike.

King Roland is worried.
He is afraid Sofia might get hurt.

"Baileywick will go along.
He will make sure you stay safe."

Sofia is ready to go.
So is Baileywick.

He was in a Groundhog troop.
"Groundhogs come prepared!" he says.

The hike begins!
Baileywick gives Sofia shade.

He clears her way.

He sweeps the path.

He keeps her cool.
Sofia wishes he would not help.

The girls stop to rest.
Baileywick pulls out a throne!
"I can sit on the ground," says Sofia.

The girls stop for water.
Sofia gets a fancy glass.

It is time to earn a badge.
The girls will build birdhouses.
Sofia gathers twigs to use.

"You might get a scratch!"
says Baileywick.
He takes the twigs from Sofia.
"I can do it myself," says Sofia.

Mrs. Hanshaw looks at
Baileywick's birdhouse.
"Sofia, *you* were supposed to
build it," she says.

Ruby and Jade get badges.
Sofia does not.

Soon Sofia has another chance.
The girls can earn a badge for
finding wood.

Baileywick is worried Sofia
will get hurt.
He beats her to every log, branch,
and twig!

Baileywick holds up the wood.
"It only counts if Sofia does it,"
Mrs. Hanshaw says.

Everyone gets a badge but Sofia.
Jade even earns a sunflower pin.

The Buttercups stop for lunch.
Baileywick cooks for Sofia.

Sofia wants to do things for herself.
"Then I can earn my last badge.
And get my sunflower pin."

Baileywick promises to leave
Sofia alone.

There is one more chance.
The girls must pick daisies
and daffodils for a badge.

They must watch out for a bad
red plant.
It gives an itchy rash.

What if Sofia touches the
bad plant?
Baileywick picks some red
flowers for her.

Baileywick's hands itch.
He needs the royal doctor.
But Baileywick cannot get down
the trail.

"We'll build a sled!" Sofia says.
She shows the Buttercups how.
The Buttercups are on their way!

Baileywick gets fixed up.
The king thanks him
for helping Sofia.

"She didn't need me at all,"
Baileywick says.
He tells how Sofia got him home.
"She's a leader, just like you."

Mrs. Hanshaw gives Sofia her badge.
Then Sofia gets a sunflower pin!
Baileywick gets something, too.
Now he is a Buttercup!

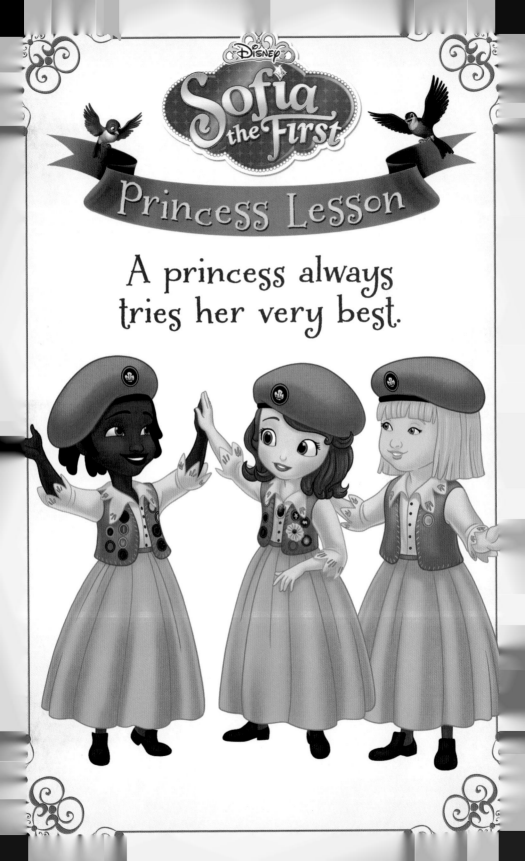